Clint Faraday
book 60
Bloody Sunrise

It was a beautiful starting day. The sunrise was clear and clean.

Then, the body in the river.

Contents

About the author

CD Moulton has traveled extensively over much of the world both in the music business, where he was a rock guitarist, songwriter and arranger and in an import/export business. He has been everything from a bar owner to auto salvage (junkyard) manager, longshoreman to high steel worker, orchid grower to landscaper, tropical fish farmer to commercial fisherman. He started writing books in 1983 and has published more than 350 books as of January 1, 2023. His most popular books to date are about research with orchids, though much of his science fiction and fantasy work has proven popular. He wrote the CD Grimes, PI series, and the Det. Nick Storie series, Clint Faraday series, and many other works.

He now resides in Gualaca, Chiriqui, Panamá, where he writes books, plays music with friends, does research with orchids and medicinal plants. He has lately become involved in fighting for the rights of the indigenous people, who are among his closest friends, and in fighting the extreme corruption in the courts and police in Panamá.

He offers the free e-book, *Fading Paradise*, that explains what he has been through because of the corruption.

CD is the discoverer of the Chadam Protocol for curing cancer.

Facebook page Ambrosia peruviana for cancer.

Unexpected Sunrise

Clint Faraday, 76, retired PI from Florida, now declared Ngobe Indio by the council, woke up and kissed his younger wife lightly, got out of bed and went into the kitchen to put on the coffee. He was addicted to the stuff, not to mention Panamanian coffee was some of the best in the world.

He went outside to stand in the middle of Dave's (his nutty musician/botanist/author) orchids at Dave's place in Gualaca to watch the faint beginning light of the sunrise. It was unexpectedly clear today. It was the rainy season, so usually had clouds in the mornings that turned to rain just before sunset. There were a couple of small fleecy clouds that were just getting the pink and gold undertones that dawn brought.

Gualaca was clean and pleasant compared to the nearby city of David.

"Hon? Are you outside?" his wife, Tyna, called.

"Yo!"

"This isn't the comarca!"

Clint never put on anything in the mornings until he decided what he was going to do that day. It was a reminder that this wasn't Quebrada Tula.

"I remembered."

Clint and Tyna were there because their daughter, Nicole, was married as of yesterday to a very good man, a Guayme Indio. They were there because the couple were married in the Indio tradition, then came to David to be "legally" married. Nicole administered the new hospital Clint and friends had built on the comarca just north of Calderas. Their son, Clintonito, called Nito, had been there, then was back in Buabidi where he was in charge of the comarca police force, such as it was. It was a new thing that such as the museum, which drew many thousands of tourists and scientists and historians, made necessary. There was a steadily growing crime rate there so the council established the legal department. It was simple pragmatism. The foreigners made it necessary, it was done.

The laws on the comarca were different than the laws elsewhere. They were simple and direct. Do this, there is a penalty, you serve or pay the penalty (and, in most cases, are banned from ever returning to the comarca). No "technicalities" or other dodges. You could get a lawyer, but that lawyer was strictly to give you advice.

It was against the law to steal. If you stole, the penalty was assessed by the council. No plea bargains for ratting out someone or whatever. All that was considered is what you stole and how it affected the one you stole from.

There were considerations for logic. If you stole rice from a market because you had no money and your family was hungry, the council would arrange for your family to have food and you were warned that a repeat would mean you were penalized. If you stole a camera or cell phone, you gave it back or paid for it and served a sentence. You knew that any repeat would mean a doubling of the sentence. If you used violence, you were going to serve a long and hard sentence, also with considerations. If it was to steal or such, you were in a heap of trouble, Boy! If it was from emotional causes, the cause was considered. If you killed someone in self defense or in defense of your family, no penalty. In defense of friends or whatever, depending on the underlying reasons. Aggressively, you would probably end up executed.

Clint thought what would happen to all those corrupt bureaucrats and politicians acting under that system and grinned. There weren't any politicians and damned few bureaucrats. What's the question?

He went back inside when he heard his cellular tone. Very few people had that number. It was his "business" phone.

"Clint Faraday?"

"Yes?"

"I am Samy Comacho with the police in Gualaca. I have a report here that tells me I may call you for aid in certain cases. I saw you here last evening so hoped I could request that you help with something that we found this morning."

"Depends on what you found."

"A body. In the river just before the town. Changuinola road."

"An accident ... you wouldn't be calling me. Murder?"

"He was stabbed through the heart and pushed into the river."

"That's what I would tend to call murder."

"Me, too!"

"That's very close. Are you there?"

"Yes."

"About ten minutes to walk. I'll be there."

<u>*The Body*</u>

"You can see he was about thirty five years old, probably part gringo or German or something. There is no identification. He was seen in town last evening. He arrived by the bus from David, but he got on it in Chiriqui. I, of course, haven't been able to check further. It was the bus that left Chiriqui at six ten last evening. He was found less than an hour ago. An Indio by the name of Santos Icarias was sleeping off a night in the Mirador under the bridge. He saw or heard nothing, but the body was right there on the stump.

"Moises was walking by on his way to work. Moises Duarte. He cleans the park every morning. Santos called to him and he came to the station when he went to work. Santos didn't know he was stabbed or he would have come himself. He thought someone had fallen from the bridge, hit the stump and was dead. Sad, but part of life.

"Antonio was at the station to report the problem with Marcheska Jimenez. She took a woman's groceries from the bus. You know how she's not right in the head – no, but she's a local character. Tonio made her give the groceries back and she hit him with a stick there. I wish we could do something, but she's not responsible.

"Anyhow, when Moises said the dead man was wearing a bright blue-green shirt and black bluejeans Tonio said he was on the bus from Chiriqui. We can assume with very strong reservations that he came to Chiriqui on the Panamá bus and was robbed here. The reservations are because of a couple of things, such as he had thirty one dollars and thirty six cents in his pocket and was wearing an expensive watch and a gold chain. Add that the closest bar is the Mirador. Moises would have noticed if there was any stranger drinking there. The Soberana isn't far, but wasn't open past seven last evening. There is still some body warmth, telling us he hasn't been dead more than two and a half hours, I'd estimate.

"Santos said you were in town, that you were in the Mirador earlier. I have heard much of you. I called."

"Because you don't believe it was a simple robbery for one split second," Clint said. "I agree. Someone killed him and took his identification, but not money or jewelry. He was killed because of some other reason."

"Yes. We are told that by the fact that only identification was taken *from the body.* He didn't come here from Panamá City or wherever with no baggage whatever. I have to speak with Moises. I have already contacted the department to check all buses and taxis that came to Chiriqui before five o'clock last evening.

"I left a message for Moises to call me. He is having his breakfast in David soon and will call."

Clint nodded and went to check over the body. The CSI team had to come from David and would be there in about twenty five minutes. Samy knew Clint had the training – had even taught some newer things to the Panamanian CSI – and wouldn't chance doing any damage to evidence there.

After a cursory check Clint said he was probably Colombian from features or his parents were from Colombia. He worked inside, mostly. His color and toning said he was an office worker or shop worker. There was a burn on his arm in a pattern that suggested a stove. He was, Clint would guess, a restaurant worker, probably a cook. He was toned to suggest he worked out, but not on a regular schedule. That was possibly work-related. He carried heavy packages or something a couple of times a week. His legs were not as muscular as his upper body, but the muscle was fairly hard. He walked a lot. Possibly, he rode a bicycle, which would explain the difference in upper body toning and different lower body toning. The jewelry and state of the hands and fingernails and shoes suggested he was not wealthy, but not poor. He didn't own wherever he worked unless it was a marginal business.

There was contrast there. The carrying of weight suggested he worked for someone else, but other things said he was a boss. Possibly, he was someone who owned and operated a small restaurant.

"Hmm. Hair well-kept, but a little long for the style here. Not from David. Possibly around the Chitre area or that kind of thing. The clothes were good, but not top of the line.

"Did you check ... no, that's for CSI. I think he has a money belt. I can ... yes. Some money or papers in it, but not a lot. Maybe we should wait to have the team tell us what's there.

"Is there good coffee anywhere close? I'm not worth a damn until I've had my third cup."

"You can take the truck. Bring us all coffee. There's an urn and foam cups at the station that we carry to these places, but there wasn't any coffee in it this morning. Juanita will have it brewed by now."

Clint agreed and took the truck to the station. He waited ten minutes for the coffee to finish brewing and for Juanita to pour out a small pot for herself, then he went back to the bridge. The CSI team came as they were drinking coffee and Clint explained what he had found and theorized. Eduardo was head of that team. Clint had taught a class in CSI that he attended. He said Clint was thoroughly competent and was authorized to investigate the money belt or anything else. He was there because the police called him, thus was officially on duty.

The money belt had a little more than two hundred dollars and a few papers ... such as a receipt made out to "The Veladero" restaurante, Veraguas. Eduardo grabbed the computer and had the restaurante checked out. It was owned by a Roberto Tomás and an Eladio Ramirez.

He brought up Roberto Tomás: 62. Panamanian. Poor health. Pensionado.

Eladio Ramirez F. was 31, a competition cyclist, Panamanian mother, Brasilian father. Neither was known nor suspected to be in any way tied to illegal activities.

"So. He was Eladio Ramirez," Samy said. "I am so disappointed! You said Colombian and it is Brasilian!"

Clint gave him the finger.

Eduardo brought up a picture for the restaurante health certificate card on the computer. It was definitely their victim. The fingerprint was on the certificate. He made a comparison. ID confirmed.

"BT and conditions say three hours to three and a quarter. Lividity says he was killed and was on his back for a short while before being tossed onto that stump. I wish he hadn't been moved, but there doesn't seem to be any loss of evidence because of it other than the body position and surrounding close clues."

"I have photographs of everything," Samy said. "I took all that, but couldn't be absolutely certain he was dead. Moises and I brought him here. He was dead, but had already been moved. Nothing has been disturbed around the stump, but I don't think there's anything there."

Eduardo and Clint both agreed. They spent awhile there, then Samy and Clint went to the station and Moises went to work. The team would handle the scene and the body. Clint noted that Samy took a video of the scene and action – and that he was very careful to include all the gawkers and vehicles. He had a rookie officer there for training who he assigned to directing traffic. He was efficient about making most of the people leave. The ones who came in vehicles. He said they were obstructing traffic and would be fined if they didn't move on. A news truck came and was about to become a problem blocking the north lane. Clint and Samy went to them and got an argument. Clint explained that he would make them a bit of the news on all other stations if they refused to comply with an order to remove their illegal blockage to traffic. They would also sit in the jail in Gualaca for six or eight hours while they were investigated. It would take so long because the police were involved in a murder investigation that their actions were impeding, meaning the police couldn't spare the personnel to process them any faster.

They got the point. They moved to the side of the road and came back with a portable camera and microphone. They might challenge Samy, but knew better than to anger Clint Faraday. His reputation for using the law better than they could preceded him.

Moises called when they were at the station. Ramirez was carrying a box that seemed heavy, but wasn't large. He also had a maleta that was also fairly heavy. The box was one of those sopa China boxes. It was taped up with about three times the masking tape more than was necessary. There were two of those tiny padlocks on the maleta.

Samy called Tole. The police checkpoint there would have certainly looked in a locked maleta!

He hadn't gone through the checkpoint.

Clint thought. He had one case where a man and his wife went along a rough rocky sideroad around the checkpoint. It wasn't well-known, but it was there. Anyone could know about it.

"Samy, call Veraguas and see when was the last time anyone saw him there. See if he got a direct bus to Santiago."

Samy nodded and made the call. He would get a call-back in ten minutes.

Samy answered the radio eight minutes later. Ramirez had taken a bus to Santiago two days before at four o'clock in the afternoon. He had gone directly to the express bus to David. That meant he went around the checkpoint about seven thirty at night. He would catch the bus to Chiriqui at the crossroad past the checkpoint. All the buses from Tole, Santiago, Soloy, San Felix or any other between eight thirty night before last until six o'clock last evening had to be checked to see if anyone remembered seeing him.

"We know who he was and where he was from and when. That will just be corroborative information," Samy said. "We have to know what he was ... Clint, perhaps he took a room here. Perhaps that is there? The maleta and box?"

Clint nodded. "It would have to be the Pensión Nueva Florida. Let's hope we get a break!"

Earl, at the pensión, said Ramirez checked in, but left nothing in the room. He left the room at about eight o'clock to find a place to get something to eat. Earl told him about the restaurant in town and the one at Fundadores. He thought he went to Fundadores. The food there was good while the food at the restaurant across from the bomberos was average. He returned about nine. Earl didn't know anything more. He had gone to the China on the main highway to get some new fixtures, then to the Estrela Bar for a couple of beers and didn't know when Ramirez left or what he was carrying. No one else was at the place so no one saw him.

They checked the room over. There wasn't anything there other than a couple of business cards left on the nightstand. They were from lawyers in David and Bocas. Changuinola.

"Samy, we are in Gualaca. You work here, I'm staying at Dave's place. He lives here. Why was Ramirez here? Was some kind of meeting set up or was he here to not be found?"

"I see. If he was here not to be found, then someone *not* from here found him. If he was to meet someone here ... then he would not be staying at this pensión in any likely scenario. Whoever found him had to stay around a while so will have been noted. The officers stationed here note any strangers or vehicles that are not here often.

"Clint? Perhaps he called someone. A lawyer. Those cards on the table were not the ones he wanted.

"Did the ... there was a celular in his pocket. The phone was wet. It will be ruined."

"But the SIM card will have the numbers he called unless he erased them. Maybe that will be our break. This didn't turn out to be one."

"Unless we consider that we found this evidence here?"

"Just possibly."

Samy called the CSI team on the computer when they got back to the station and said he had to have the celular found on the body. Karla said she had already copied everything on the SIM. It was in the comp. It was suddenly on the screen, so Samy saved it.

"It lists the last twenty numbers called and the times. It will be one of the last seven, which were all made yesterday after five o'clock PM. I will call them from the computer and record what is learned."

He punched the first: "Habla."

"Quien habla?" In Panamá the question (who are you?) is a normal thing to ask when someone answers a phone. In the states, most would hang up.

"Gina Morales. Que?"

"I am trying to locate Eladio Ramirez. Do you know where he is?"

"I don't even know *who* he is." She hung up.

"Quien habla"

"Licenciado Alberto Lewis. How can I help you?"

Clint pointed to a card and shook his head.

"Mi culpa." Samy rang off.

"Ola! Que?"

"Quien habla?"

"Marta. Que?"

"I am trying to locate Eladio Ramirez. Is he there?"

"No. He is that man from Veraguas? He wanted me to ... what I do. He says I charge too much, but I always say you get better when you pay better. I am good!"

"Gracias." He rung off. "A prostitute. Tower number is in Las Lomas."

"Your dime. Que?"

"Quien habla?"

"Renaldo. What you want? I ain't got much. Should have some tomorrow."

Samy raised an eyebrow.

"Crack? Not the cheap crap!"

Clint shook his head.

"Tomorrow. Maybe after two. All I got now my dog would piss on if I offered it."

"Eladio said you had some good stuff. I'll call tomorrow."

"Eladio who? I ain't got no client named Eladio. I only know one Elad ... fuck you!" he hung up.

"Number one! Where?" Clint asked.

"Las Lomas tower."

"I wonder if maybe that lawyer was in Las Lomas!" Clint got the card. The office address was in David. Las Lomas is a suburb.

"Maybe we can concentrate on Las Lomas. That would remove a lot of prime suspects – if we had any!"

"G. G. Garcia, Licenciado, Especialidad in casos criminales. How can I be of service?"

Clint looked at the other card and said it wasn't the same one.

"I am with the police in Gualaca. A Mr. Ramirez has died. I wish to know who to contact, as he had no identification with him.

We found his name through fingerprints. This and a couple other numbers were on a note in his pocket."

"Ramirez is a common name?"

"It's, uh, Eladio Ramirez. Address is Veraguas."

"I see. I am not at liberty to give you any information about a client without ... you say he is dead?"

"Yes. Murdered."

"I see. I can give you no information over the telephone. I can give you very little not on the telephone, but there might possibly be an item or two I could discuss with you in person if you are truly the police and have autoritification of that identity."

"You are aware of a police specialist named Clint Faraday?"

"Anyone in law in this country will know about Mr. Faraday. He has humiliated myself in court, though I hold no enmity. He did his job, I did mine. My client lied to me. It is a loss due to the client's cause."

"He is acting as a special consultant. Will you speak with him?"

"In person, certainly."

"Where are you?"

"Just east of Las Lomas on the CPA. By the large Accel station. It is possible I am watched. I know this celular isn't overheard. We must meet in what will seem a chance encounter. Not too close to this office."

"Do you know the restaurant next to the bombas in Chiriqui on the CPA?"

"Yes. I eat there sometimes when I have business there."

"Half an hour?"

"I will be there." He rung off.

"I would tend to think that, just perhaps, we have our break!" Samy said. "I would also think it were better to wait before we call the other numbers. They were called after the one to Garcia. Maybe we will have a clue as to what we're looking for."

"We can hope. I'll get my car and meet Garcia. It wouldn't be a good idea to use a police vehicle. It would be suspicious as hell for me to show up in anything else."

Clint went to Dave's to tell Tyna where he was going and what was happening. She said it would really seem unlikely that he would meet with someone in secret if he had his wife along. She liked that restaurant. It was lunch time.

He didn't ever want Tyna exposed to danger from his cases, but there wouldn't be any danger from this. It really would make the meeting seem coincidental.

Clint parked to the side and he and Tyna went in to sit at a table to the side where he parked. He could be seen from the entrance, but wouldn't appear to be trying to be seen.

Garcia didn't know Tyna would be there. It might make him leery of making contact.

Clint looked around, using his very good peripheral vision that would make it appear he was looking somewhere else. Judging from the choice of words and the sound of the voice, Garcia wasn't there.

He and Tyna ordered a typical lunch and sat to chat a bit. A Mercedes pulled in up front and a somewhat fat, impeccably dressed man got out and came inside. Two people greeted him. They called him "GG" and he waved at them. He spotted Clint and walked past to the counter. Clint nodded when he passed. He went a few feet farther, then stopped to turn back. He came to the table to announce just loud enough for anyone close to hear that he was a lawyer who Clint had once, several years ago, made a fool out of in court, much to his client's distress.

No hard feelings! That was a client he was almost forced to defend! The stupid moron lied to everyone, including his lawyer, which is done by fools and idiots, of which he was both.

"Oh, yes! That thing where the man who was exposing corrupt border police was murdered. I remember.

"Join us?"

"Why, thank you! It would be an honor! I'll order!"

He put a small tablet and a couple of pens on the table, managing to have a finger pointed to a slip on a clip as he put the things down, turned, and headed for the counter. Clint leaned to talk with Tyna, using his peripheral talent to note when two large blacks came from the far side entrance to an empty table just to Clint's rear. One was very big and had dredlocks and gold chains and fancy rings. The other was almost as big and looked more toward the Latino, so was probably a mestizo.

Clint and Tyna talked for a minute until Garcia returned carrying a tray. He asked Tyna to move the tablet so he could sit the tray down. She carelessly dropped the tablet on the other empty chair, not even looking at it. Clint didn't see her do it, but the tablet was laying there minus the slip. Clint managed to point to the blacks with his thumb where they couldn't see it.

"Are you on a police case – that you may speak of, of course – now?" Garcia asked.

"Well, yes and no. There's a body we identified, but there was no identification on it. The only thing you could call a clue was a cell phone that had been in the water. We called what numbers survived, but only got a drug dealer and a couple of prostitutes. And a lawyer who said he didn't know who the hell this Ramirez was. Samy, the cop in Gualaca, said it was a waste of time to call those numbers. He mostly lost interest when he got the drug dealer. There's no way the police are going to solve drug hits. I know I'm too old and don't have that much time to waste, myself.

"You got anymore corrupt politicians and police to defend?"

"Well, corrupt and politician – and far too often, police – are synonyms, aren't they?"

"It sometimes seems like it." He didn't think it would be diplomatic to include lawyers. He did that mentally.

They chatted about nothing for awhile. Tyna and Clint had a delicious flan-based dessert with Garcia ("My treat!"), then went to their car. Clint said, "The blacks. Table behind me!" quickly as they waved goodbye. Garcia nodded just enough to let Clint know they were involved.

Clint and Tyna got in the car and headed on toward David. Garcia went down the road toward Chorcha. It would look like Clint stopped on the way to somewhere and Garcia had an appointment in back of Chiriqui.

Clint called Samy and said he would be there soon. He had to read something, then would decide what to do.

Tyna handed him the slip. It had a little impression from something that was written on the page over it. Clint laid it on the dash in the faint dust there, then slid it lighhtly, then looked at it.

rio Jalisco 555-0005 He unfolded it to see what it said:

6 mil efv dg mny

dtr rst bsra

tcdo

ll ct ltr

jmcno colno bscr

<u>Amenisado! Cuidado!</u>

"It would seem Ramirez found six million dollars in cash. It's drug money. It was ... detras ... behind the garbage cans at the restaurant. He took it. I don't ... ll. Llama ... call for date later.

A Jamaican and a Colombian were searching for him. Garcia was threatened. Be careful.

"You know what this means?"

Tyna looked thoughtful. "What means?"

"The fact the Jamaican and the Colombian were in that restaurant."

"They didn't get the money. They wonder if Garcia can lead them to it."

"Nobody ever said *you* were slow!"

"He's damned clever, Clint! Don't let him use you! He really might be able to lead them to it."

"I don't think so. If he could, he wouldn't let me in on it for anything. He thinks I can lead him to it."

"Can you?"

"Not at the moment, but maybe I can figure it.

"You know something?"

"What?"

"I want to know where Eladio got his dinner."

"You don't make sense, but that's nothing new."

"If he ate at Fundadores, he might have seen something. Dave has taken a lot of pictures for his book covers there and was collecting aluminum back of the place and down to the river there. I've seen a few pictures that give me an idea.

"We can't do anything today. It'll wait until tomorrow. I don't think it will get personally dangerous – unless I do find that money. If I do, you have to get away from here."

"I'd say, 'Clint! Be careful!' – but you'd just say that was used up in some old TV series about Matt Dillon or somebody such."

"Well? It *was*!"

"So. I take it you're going to have a beer or two at Fundadores this afternoon?"

"Uh-huh."

"Atlas, Lili!" Clint ordered. Only the barmaid and cook and a man who hung around a lot were there.

"Hi, Clint. Haven't seen you around for awhile. You in on our little murder?"

"In a small way. It doesn't look like anything that would interest me to any extent. It looks like a drug thing. Those are hopeless.

"Did he have dinner here? Earl said he sent him."

"He ate around six and left, then came back about nine thirty or so. I thought he took the Changuinola bus, that one that comes by about a quarter after ten. He had a backpack on when he left about then. He went toward the China. That's where most people wait for the late buses. I guess he went on to the Mirador. I thought he was probably robbed, but the backpack was old and he didn't look like he had anything to rob for."

"We thought that at first. Samy found some kind of clue that makes it look like drugs, but you never know."

"Samy found something about drugs? That would be why that big Jamaican, Mambo, was asking about him. If I ever saw anyone who looked like he should be a drug runner in those Jamaican movies, he would be it!"

"Yeah. I saw him in a restaurant in Chiriqui. Scary type."

"Speak of Satan and he appears!" she cried as a fancy Jaguar pulled into the drive.

Clint felt he would be followed. He didn't bring a weapon. He didn't think it would be needed. He suddenly wished he had! All he had on him was pepper spray.

Only the Jamaican was in the car. Where was his partner?

Following Garcia, no doubt.

"Well, he may be involved, but I sort of doubt it. A couple things make me wonder."

"Yeah! You see him in a restaurant in Chiriqui, then come here and there he comes. Why is he following you?"

"Maybe I'll ask him."

"He was here last night. I saw that car two times. Once by the park and once at the big China," the regular customer said. "If he was following me I wouldn't ask him *nothing*!"

"But you aren't Clint Faraday," Lili short back. "Clint, Dario. He comes around sometimes. We say he's our bad news man. Every time he's around something bad happens. Look at now!"

They all laughed.

The black came to order a Balboa. Clint figured there wasn't anything to lose, so said, "Mambo? Why are you following me? If you have something to say, just say it."

"What makes you think I'd waste my time following you, old man? You senile?"

"Gee! I'm in a restaurant in Chiriqui, there you are! You make it a point to sit almost on top of me! I come here for a beer, there you come! I'm stupid!

"What do you want?"

"Okay. I wasn't following you in Chiriqui. I was following your lawyer friend. He met you. Now I want to know why."

"I don't have any lawyer friends. Do you mean Garcia?"

"What was that about?"

"I had a case where his client was found guilty of corruption. His client had lied to him. He fell right into a trap because of that and ended up looking like a fool. As he said, he was just doing his job, I was just doing mine. If the client had been honest we wouldn't have been in that courtroom and the client would have had to serve four years. As it was, he got six on one count and two on a count I wouldn't have even mentioned. He said it was almost funny when he looked back on it. He learned a lot from it."

"He wasn't after the money?"

"Money? A lawyer is *always* after the money. It's the psychology behind most of them even studying law and trickery. What kind of question is that?"

"I could like you! No shit and don't back down from anything!

"If you aren't ... I think you probably have it figured something like it is. Ramirez stole a lot of money from some people it is not wise to steal from. A *lot* of money. Cash. Six million dollars. We don't know what he did with it. He talked with Garcia on the phone and told him about it. A person heard the conversation. Garcia might know where the money is. We want it back."

"Six million bucks? Garcia would have it and be in Venezuela with it if he knew anything. Why bother with someone so easy to figure?"

"I don't think he knows where too exactly, only that Ramirez had it with him and didn't when they found his body."

"I see. You killed him trying to find where the money is and don't have any way to find it now. It's obvious Garcia doesn't know where it is. I met with Garcia and am known to be able to find things, so you figure I know where to find it."

"It's a lot of money. Do you know?"

"I could probably figure it, but I don't care about any money. Look where it got Ramirez. Look where it's getting you. Just a 'maybe' gets Garcia in hot water. It's not worth it."

"I was told you have a few million yourself."

"A few. It's in a corporation. It can do something that way. My lifestyle doesn't put much stock in money."

"Clint got more than that on the one case in Puerto Armuelles, didn't you?" Lili asked.

"That was a long time ago. Something like that."

"The pirate treasure, you got more than that. The museum thing, you could ask the chief for a couple of billion and he'd give it to you."

"No, he wouldn't. He wouldn't give me much at all. It's not his to give. You don't understand the Indio philosophy. If I, or any Ngobe, have a real need, it's there. That belongs to us, not to me. We use it for projects for all the people. Schools and clinics and roads and whatever everyone uses. You can't understand the culture. There are very few things that an individual owns. It's not like that. You have exclusive use of the house your family lives in and first rights to vegetables or whatever around that house, but even most of that is comunal. It's an 'us' society, not a 'me' society. 'Ours' not 'mine'. I can't explain so anyone of a different culture can understand."

"Comunism?"

"In a pure sense. Not Marxism or Stalinism or Maoism, which had almost nothing to do with communism."

An oversized monstrosity of a Hummer pulled into the lot. Two obvious thugs got out of the back and a large bull of an individual wearing an Armani suit that still didn't fit him right and an angry scowl came out and marched into the place. Clint grinned at him.

"Ivan? I know your brother. We've talked on the phone. What's this bullshit about a few lousy million dollars? You wouldn't bother to notice something like that. It's one night out slumming on the town."

"You have spoken...? You know Vasily? Who are you?"

"Clint Faraday."

"Ah! Yes! Then I won't have to pull the silly bigshit mob boss act! You know it's false!

"Mambo, why didn't you tell me it was Clint you called me here to meet and scare into telling you where Jefe's, as Clint said, lousy shit six million dollars are?

"Clint, it isn't about the money, it's about why the money was where it was when it was. Mambo's boss is afraid it tells something about some people and much more important things could be lost if a certain leak isn't repaired."

"I remember advice from Vasily about that kind of thing. He said, when you know that a certain section of pipe is leaking you would be wise to replace the entire section. Cut it away and put a shiny new section to take its place.

"For Mambo's part, he also said that only an idiot kills the person with information you need. A corpse can't give you information – as Ramirez has pointed out."

"I didn't kill him! Perez didn't kill him! We don't know who did!" Mambo protested. "That's what has my boss and some others very worried! We would get the money back and he would answer a few questions, then we would just scare him into staying shut up. Maybe give him ten grand to clam."

"Ah! I see! And nobody wanted me to know the real reasons," Ivan said. "I can fully guarantee there was no leakage nor subterfuge from our end. That leaves only two other possibilities, doesn't it?"

"Two others not in Panamá?" Clint asked.

"Unfortunately they are both in Panamá," Ivan replied. "We will try to handle this with minimum disturbance elsewhere. We might request your help. It will be for the good of Panamá."

"I know I can trust you. I'll do what I can. I'll need information."

"Then we will meet elsewhere in a place we can be absolutely certain has no little holes that could leak.

"Now! We sing and dance and have a few beers and maybe a little vodka.

"Is your weird musician friend still alive ... he would be ninety something years old now, so I guess not."

"Dave's still around. I'm staying at his place here."

"We will later go there. For now, drinks for everyone! Girlie, play some music. Rock and romantic. Marco Antonio Solis. Mana. Shakira, but her older stuff. Some English. Guns and Roses and Elton John and U-two."

He gave Lili a twenty dollar bill. She called a boy about ten years old to say to play the kind of music they wanted. He knew the juke box. He would have to go to the filling station for quarters. She didn't have but two in the cash register. Ivan laughed and told a thug to bring a couple rolls of quarters from the glove box. Lili tried to hand back the twenty. He said she could have it for being so pretty.

It turned into a fun kind of night. Perez came in at about ten thirty, announcing Garcia hadn't known shit about anything and that he'd been wasting his time to be worrying about the idiot. If he'd found the money, he wouldn't have had a clue as to what to do with it even if he had only gotten part of it.

Clint figured he knew about where the money would be hidden. He sneaked away for a few minutes, went around behind the rodeo grounds parking lot and returned, carrying the backpack and a box. He handed it to Ivan, who gave it to Mambo, who gave it to Perez.

Just before they closed the place for the night Ivan opened the box. It was packed with plain paper stacks that were cut to the size and shape of bills. Ivan found that hilarious. Mambo brought the backpack. That did have bills. Hundred dollar bills. A million and a half. Ivan was suddenly not so happy about it.

Mambo looked like he would faint when the money wasn't there. Perez had a studied, "Oh, well, that's the way it goes!" look. He also looked more than a little scared. He was trying to hide that. The Dario character was a little drunk. He said, "I can guess some shithead's ass will be in a crack over that!"

"You're here. Something else bad when you're here," Lili said.

"And where was it secreted that our very professional comrades could not discover?"

"In the garbage pile by the trail to the project road where it belongs. Pull the top layer back, toss it there, throw some garbage on top with the vines rolled back into place so it looks like nothing was moved for the past month. Simple."

"Clint, my dear friend, I think this answers some questions. I will go to David for the night, then we will meet tomorrow to attempt to fathom exactly what who is doing to whom. We must puzzle out some disturbing things. It is not that there was paper in the box or that there was money in the backpack. It is because of both things."

"It points in two directions at once, huh?"

"Exactly! Both may be true!"

Clint was up before dawn. Ivan wouldn't be up until ten. They would meet there where Clint would take him somewhere they wouldn't decide until they were there.

Clint knew how to drink and knew when he had enough. He didn't have the loggy feeling or a hangover. He remembered every detail of the night before. He felt the same as usual. Mambo came by and got his boss on the phone. Clint talked to "Jefe" a few minutes, explaining what he thought Jefe should know. He talked with Mambo about who might have killed Ramirez. He didn't know. It could be something ordered by either of two groups.

Perez came from the side road to park around the corner behind some crotons, which Clint noticed with his peripheral vision talent. The Dario character from Fundadores was walking by and said something to him. He pointed at Clint and shook his head. Dario shrugged and went on.

"It might be very important. Did Ramirez start out with the money in that box and end up with it being gone?"

"So far as I know, yes. He certainly wouldn't have taken the money out, so I can't figure that."

"As far as you know?"

"The money was in the box when Perez left it back there. I saw him put it in the car and I saw him take it out and around the back. I was sure it was the right box because Perez wrapped it with about ten times the tape it needed. He said he wanted to be damned sure it didn't split open or something if anyone dropped it. We took it right out and put it in the trunk, drove to the restaurant and put it where Jefe said. Another party was supposed to get it the next morning before the restaurant opened. Ramirez was early and took out the garbage and found it. That put Perez and me in a bad spot, but Jefe knows he can trust us. He just wants the money back. It was a payment for some ... stuff."

"Think carefully. Was the box you opened here different in any way than the box you saw Perez put back there?"

"It looked the same to me. It was the one he put in the trunk, I'm ... almost positive."

"Almost? That means you have some kind of strong suspicion."

"I'm sure!"

"It could get you both killed. This has already gotten one person removed."

"Faraday ... well, it was just that ... well, there was more tape ... I mean, it was so much that I could be wrong, but ... the piece on the top was ... I thought it was straight across on the box when we ... he put it in the trunk. The one we opened last night had a sort of ... angle, you know?"

"Liam Perez wrapped the box in the beginning in Veraguas. *He* wrapped a lot of tape straight across. *He* put it in the trunk of *his* car. *He* took it out and put it behind the restaurant. It was found by someone else. You traced that person to Gualaca. He was killed. I found where he hid the money. The box was wrapped just a little differently when I found it.

"Why was part of it in the backpack? That seems odd."

"It wasn't. There were two boxes. It was in a smaller box. I think Ramirez took it out and put it in the backpack."

"You know damned well what this has to mean."

"It means Liam switched part of the money. He killed Ramirez and hoped no one would ever find it.

"Clint! He would have to know he can't get away with it! It could cause a war! My god! Two other groups will be trying to get us!"

"Which leads me to wonder about another thing or two. I have to discuss it with Ivan. It can be very important to him."

"I don't see how, but you're a long way ahead of me on this one. What should I do? Should I tell Jefe?"

"Not yet. Let us try to work something out. Don't be anywhere around Perez when there aren't several others around."

"He'll see he's been figured and might want to start finding a way out of a corner. If it's through me, tough shit!"

"If this is what it looks like, there aren't any corners. A circle doesn't have corners. He'll try to kill off anyone who can finger him in any way. Don't be where he can. If it comes right down to the wire, remember that he intends to kill you. You don't owe him any consideration whatever. He's gone a long way to make it possible to make you the goat if he's figured. He would have to say he killed you when you attacked him when he faced you with the fact you were the one who did the switch. He can't see why he couldn't do that until too late. If you expect it, you can turn it on him. I don't think you'd be squeamish about knocking over someone who plans to knock you over. Don't give a hint you know anything."

"He can't do it and get away with it?"

"No. You can't unring a bell. That one was loud and long. He shouldn't have tried ... maybe I'll have to talk to Jefe! Maybe this circle has gotten a bit complicated!

"Mambo, I think you're not so bad. Get the hell out. Go somewhere none of them can find you."

"But ... then when he says I was the one it will look like ... I can't think!"

"No. I said the bell was rung. When he tries that dodge I'll have him in a vice he can't squirm out of! Trust me!"

"I don't know where to go! They know every place I do!"

"I have a friend. You can bet they won't look for you there. You'll have to stay out of sight for about a week. That should be time enough. You can't take that car."

"Fuck the car! What good is it if I'm dead? Perez will see me drive away and know something's happening he didn't plan on. He's where he can see us right now. I think you know that."

"Do you have a way to communicate with him I'm not going to catch?"

"I can call him from my car. Walky-Talky."

"Okay. I'll get them to concentrate on me and Ivan. You get the hell out. Tell him you couldn't find which way we were going, so you'll be waiting just around a corner toward that way and he can watch this way. You don't know which car we'll take. He can see so call you as soon as he knows. If you're still in range, ask him which way we're heading. It will be that way, so he'll have to follow. You can do something to make it look like the radio is going out or something. It should be too late for him to follow you by then.

"Take the bus to Chiriqui, then get the one to Soloy. I'll give you a note to give to the driver and door boy. The Soloy bus will pass the corner there every hour and a half. If you can time it right you can be there and gone before they know anything about it.

"No! Drive your car to Chiriqui and up the road half a kilometer to the truck repair yard. Leave it with Francisco there. I'll give you a note for him. He can take you to one of several places where you can get the bus for Soloy. No one will remember seeing you on that bus, I guarantee.

"Soloy is in the comarca. You're black. It might be hard. Be a friend and they'll treat you like a friend."

He nodded. Clint said he knew the car Perez was driving was around the corner. "Go the other way when you leave here. Wait until the Hummer comes. We'll talk for a couple of minutes here to give you time to radio Perez about not knowing which way. Perez will have to watch that. It'll give you some time. I'll try to get Ivan to help me distract Perez."

They chatted awhile. Perez was sitting there watching. The woman from across the road came to chat a minute. The Dario character came by, a little drunk already. He ignored Perez. He turned right and stopped to say something to the woman. Clint said it was business. He staggered on. Mambo shook his head. "Lili said something bad happens every time he comes around. I believe it! He's a living bad luck charm!"

The neighbor said, "He's very rich, but he's a ladron! Nobody likes him. He used to be a politician and was caught taking bribes." She waved and went back to her house.

Ivan came twenty minutes later. Clint quickly told him what he planned and said he would explain what he was suspecting after Mambo was safely gone. He had learned a few things that could tie this thing up pretty quickly. Mambo drove off and Ivan stood by the Hummer, talking to Clint, until he had time to get out of Gualaca, but Clint didn't think Perez would take any chances now. Not with Ivan there. He wouldn't be able to explain leaving when Clint and Ivan were right there in plain sight. He could play his games when there wasn't a player there who could use a distraction to his own advantage. Ivan was far to big a chance to take. If he missed something there it wouldn't be explainable.

Ivan talked to his bodyguards for a couple of minutes. They got in the Hummer and turned it around to head back up the road. Clint saw Perez start his engine and edge toward the corner. Clint made it obvious that Ivan was going with him in his car. It would look like Ivan was in the Hummer to someone from a distance, but Perez would see it as a subterfuge to get any followers to go after the Hummer. Theoretically, anyone would follow that. Perez was where he could see what was happening and would follow Clint's car.

And get a hell of a shock!

Clint and Ivan went toward Bocas on the main carretera. When they were in La Mina Clint turned off the main highway and headed down the steep road into the town and through toward Hornitos. The guys in the Hummer said Perez had hesitated before heading down that road. It took a hell of a good driver to manipulate the twists and turns on such a steep grade. Clint knew the road intimately and knew where he could get up a little speed, forcing Perez to take some scary chances.

They came into Hornitos where the road became far easier. Clint pulled in front of a little restaurant. He and Ivan went in and sat at a table to order hojaldres and coffee. They got orders of bolitas and huevos revueltos and hidago and sat to talk. They had discussed what had happened with a lot of side paths to personal things and with some theories thrown in on the way from Gualaca. They didn't get into much detail or say much. Clint had spotted the celular in the back that was probably being used as a transmitter.

Most of the area didn't have any signal. Bummer! He and Ivan used their own celulars to check. There was no signal here.

"Okay. No more need for bullshit. I think you can see what I suspect," Clint said. "I think everybody has a plan. Jefe wants to start a war because he's strongest at the moment, but that could change for any number of reasons he would have no control over. Dorindo will fight with Delgado until they're both too weakened to go further, then Jefe steps in and takes over. Meanwhile, either Dorindo or Delgado made a deal. Perez does something to throw it all on one or the other so Jefe will join whoever and they become partners that the winner in that one takes over. Perez saw his chance and is going to make it impossible for Jefe or Dorindo or Delgado to stay out of it, then he takes the spoils.

"For his idea to work means he stays out of the equation so far as any of them know until the shooting starts. A statement at last night's party means he can't put it all on Mambo, as he planned. He doesn't know that or thinks we missed it. Mambo has disappeared, meaning he can say, 'See? It was him all along! That's why he ran!'

"What I didn't tell you in the car was that the box you opened last night was not the box that left Jefe's. It was wrapped in that extreme manner by *Perez*, who then took it out and put it in the trunk of *his* car where he and Mambo took it to the restaurant and *Perez* took it out of the trunk to put where Jefe said to put it while Mambo stayed in the car. Perez knew he would be asked to pack the money. *Perez* brought the sopa China box that *he* wrapped to carry in *his* car. He would have a box in the trunk that looked like the one he wrapped. He would have a few million dollars to play with. It would leave suspicion all around. No one would be able to figure what had happened.

"Then Ramirez took the garbage out early. Now no one would ever know about the substitution. Everybody's drooked asses were on the chopping block.

"Remember those last three strips of tape on the box last night? They were angled across from one side a bit toward the other?

"The box wrapped at Jefe's had no angles to the wrapping. It was subtle. Mambo noted it subconsciously and didn't remember it until I had him concentrate. He had a little nag in the back of his mind that something was out of kilter, but didn't know what.

"Until last night Perez could put almost all of it on Mambo. He would stage having to kill Mambo in some kind of phony fight about him discovering Mambo had switched the boxes. Last night before we opened the box Perez ...."

"I'll be damned! He said Garcia would only have found part of the money if he found it at all! He knew it was switched – because he switched it! He was almost smug, then looked scared. I think he realized he'd said the wrong thing! I think the last thing he expected was that I would come there in person. He could fool an employee, but he wasn't so sure he could fool me."

"And who suggested you get involved? Why?"

"Jefe. As a favor. So he was trying to set me up for knocking over the others. I do not operate in any such manner. I'm in it and he doesn't know how to get me out. He planned to take over, but so did Delgado and so did Dorindo – and so did Perez. Perez is the monkey wrench in the works for all of them.

"What a strange thing! Everybody has a plan, none of them have a chance of working unless at least one of the others is taken out! That money was supposed to be there so Jefe could start things between Delgado and Dorindo. Part of it was to be missing so Delgado or Dorindo could start things according to Perez's plan, but that came after. It wasn't supposed to be missing at all for the others until ... so it was all Perez all along. I'll be damned! It's really funny as hell, isn't it?"

"Up until Ramirez got involved. Then it got serious. Murder isn't funny."

"Now I don't understand why he was killed. He had to be alive for any of their plans to work.

"Ah! Except Perez! But Perez must *not* be the one who killed him! That would have to be put on Mambo, then it might work. It would work very well if the police could be convinced that neither Perez nor Mambo could have killed him.

That would get Dorindo and Delgado – and even Jefe! – to the boiling point, but fast!"

"But Mambo is out of reach and Perez said the wrong thing at the wrong time. He has to fight to survive now. That means getting rid of you, me, Mambo, maybe your two bodyguards. We can't hope to tie him to Ramirez's killing regardless of what we know. It's a matter of knowing it as opposed to being able to prove it."

"Oh, you missed what he said before the part about Garcia only getting part of the money?"

Clint thought for a few seconds, then a grin spread across his face. "Garcia *hadn't* known. He *had been* wasting his time. Even if he *had gotten* only a part of it.

"Garcia's dead. Perez can't get out of that one! He admitted a murder in front of a bunch of people!"

"Which will solve a part of the problem. We still have a big part to handle. I do. I hope you will aid me in it."

"Certainly! If it's not handled now it will only get bigger and worse. They'll all feel like they've gotten away with something and will get cocky, which means they'll start a more earnest type of fighting among themselves."

"If it would stay contained I would hesitate to attempt to stop it. Every half-smart hood will try to get into it, which will spread it out until innocent people are caught in the crossfire. You and Vasily and I have discussed that. We agree with you that it is too far when those not involved by their own choice are drawn in. They are the ones who are hurt most by such things. That is the point of no tolerance from the three of us."

"It'll be a matter of containing them. I don't think we can without putting it all on one of them. That lets the others off the hook, so to speak."

"I think we can work it so Perez is the one who gets the hook, bigtime! His one hope to avoid anything he couldn't at least leave a doubt about was Mambo, who is the only one of that bunch who didn't have a personal plan. He's not ambitious in the same ways as them. He just wants to get by and have a nice car and good clothes and a bunch of women who hang all over him. It's what he has. He'll be loyal to Jefe as long as jefe is loyal to him."

"I tend to like him, too. He's rather refreshingly basic. He's not too bright, but he's sincere and loyal.

"What do we do now?"

"Perez is between the devil and the deep blue sea at the moment and doesn't know it. We have to figure a way to use that."

"What do you mean?"

"How many places did you see on the way down here where a car can pull off the road to where it can't be seen from that road?"

Ivan stared hard at Clint a moment, then an evil smirk crossed his face. "Ah! We're the deep blue sea. My Hummer's the devil. Felix would have contacted me if Perez didn't stop somewhere on the way where he could see us and we couldn't see him. There is no such place. He is sitting right up there by that television relay tower. You can see the reflection on his windshield. The Hummer will be above him where he is in view.

"Shall we leisurely stroll to your car and turn around to head back up the incline? He will do the same to stay out of sight ahead of us. He should have no trouble. That thing he's driving has a lot of power your car doesn't.

"The Hummer will not turn around and head back up. He will be in a vice."

"We don't know his firepower!" Clint warned.

"Very true. He doesn't know ours. Perhaps you have nothing in your car. I can assure you there is enough in the Hummer to stand off an army!"

"Okay!" Clint got in and started the engine. "Wagons-ho-o!" Ivan giggled.

The Hummer was blocking the road on a curve with a drop of who knows how many meters to the right and a straight up wall of rock to the left. The Porsche Perez was driving couldn't get around it. He couldn't back down that steep grade. He was caught and knew it. He got out and stood with his hands on his head.

"Let me handle this one. I know how. I want to learn some things," Ivan said. Clint nodded.

Ivan sat to seem to be chatting with Clint while Perez stood there with his hands behind his head. Ivan's thugs seemed to act like they were used to this, that Ivan would come out and give orders when he was damned good and ready and not before.

"He's pissing in his pants by now. It's going to get worse and worse," Ivan said. He waited another minute, then opened the door and started out, turned to Clint, and said, "You should have heard him whine!" and laughed in a crazy sort of wild way. He got out of the car, looked around, and said. "I love this cool mountain air. The food's one hell of a lot better tasting up here.

"I like food, as you can see! It's not full of a bunch of shit to keep it from spoiling up here. That shit also keeps it from being digested."

He went to the edge of the road and looked over. "It's, what? Sixty meters before there's anything but rocks. Almost straight down. If you fell off of up here you'd bounce a bit!"

He leaned out some and shook his head. "I wonder what kind of splut a body'd make if it fell this high and hit that big rock down there. You could probably hear it up here. I sure as all hell wouldn't climb down there just for that.

"I'm just killing time. I don't want to go back into David and listen to the shit from that bunch of stupid wannabe clowns and their silly plots and plans. They have a lot of roadmaps that lead to a bridge out. About half of them are so stupid they drive right on and go over.

"Hey! Clint! Look at this! You got a camera? I want a picture!"

Clint knew he was using psychology to break Perez down. He got his camera from the glove box and went to stand beside Ivan, who pointed almost straight down. There was nothing there but a bunch of boulders.

"Don't that look like a big open door? See the way that flat one right up against that cave thing looks just like a door? It looks like a door to a giant's house, don't it?"

Clint looked where he was pointing. It really did look like a big stone door!

"Yeah," Clint replied. "An open door to hell! I wonder! There's an old gold mine somewhere around here. That's where La Mina got the name. That may be it."

Ivan winked at Clint and whispered, "I really do want a picture." Louder, he called, "Niño! Come here and look at this! You, too, Naldo! Bring crudface. He's about stupid enough to think he could run away somewhere up here and would fall and hurt himself."

They all came to look down at the old mine entrance (if that was what it was).

"I'd bet a man could dive right through that door from up here," Ivan said. "It could be a goldmine or the door, like Clint said, to hell."

Clint said, "I guess it could be both if you dove through it from up here."

Ivan giggled. "That's a good one! Point up for Clint!

"Well, you got some pics. I can look at them when I reminisce about this place. Tourist time over! Back to business.

"Hey, Shithead! I got some questions. You got the answers. We can make a deal where you don't see if you can dive through that door maybe. I don't think it would be so pretty with a pile of shit like you blocking it."

"Jesus Christo, Mr. Armakov! I don't know anything! I just do what Jefe tells me!"

"Yeah. I'm stupid enough to think Jefe told you to switch boxes and leave the idea Dorindo or Delgado is trying to start a war – that they would see through in two seconds and think Jefe was doing it. The only one stupid enough to even try such a thing is *you*, fuckhead!"

"It wasn't me, Mr. Armakov! It was Mambo! I didn't know what he was doing! I figured it out! He's running because he did it!"

"Mambo is doing something for me. He isn't running from anything," Clint said. "He saw the tape was different on the box we opened than it was when you put it in your car to take to the restaurant. You were the only one who touched that box. We took fingerprints and yours were on that tape. Not Mambo's."

"Lots of people touched that tape! When we opened it ten people touched it!"

"Not the layer under the top. Your prints are the only ones there. You put that tape on that box," Clint said. "We're not idiots! Only an idiot wouldn't think of something so simple and obvious! You!"

"Oh, god! I'm sorry! I just wanted to help Jefe get control!"

"By getting the others gunning for him? Really?" Ivan asked.

Perez sank to his knees. "Oh, please, Mr. Armakov. He'll kill me if I talk and you will if I don't. I got nowhere to turn!"

"Tell me about it. Have some way for me to prove it. I'll get you out of Panamá and into Nicaragua. You can decide where to go from there," Clint said quickly. "There are only three ways that would ... four. I'll be damned!"

"Give it to us. I'll keep the deal, though I don't need it."

"Now you're ahead of me," Ivan said. "What do you see that I missed?"

"I see a connection from something Garcia gave me. I read a part of the message that was there if someone else saw it. The part I was supposed to get was where no one would see it who wasn't trained to look for such things. I found it, but didn't pay any attention to it. That's not like me!

"Perez! Give me the name, even though I'm sure I know it!"

"What name – like I don't know."

"Jalisco. Dario is Dario Jalisco."

"Yeah. He's in charge. I was working for him when I got in with Jefe. Nobody knows how big he is.

"You saw him this morning, right?"

"When he came by and said something to you and when he came back later, supposedly drunk, and ignored you, then came to see what Mambo and I were talking about. I was suspicious. He wasn't drunk fifteen minutes earlier and didn't have time to get drunk. He seemed drunk last night, but I watch those things. He drank three beers in four hours and one shot of vodka. He said something about somebody's ass in a crack about the missing money. He seemed happy about it so he thought us finding that would make his plan work after all.

"What? You're supposed to steer us into thinking it was under orders from Jefe, then change to saying it was Dorindo or Delgado or both?"

"All three. You don't know who he's really after."

"Me," Ivan said. "I didn't ever see him before, but I collected a lot of money that a certain bribe was to be made available. It broke an alcalde in a town. The alcalde was Dario Gonzalez Jalisco.

"Clint, you say Garcia tried to tell you that? You can be sure?"

"Let's go to the main road where my phone will work. Perez goes on to Changuinola. I'll have a friend there to get him into Costa Rica at Sixola. Another friend in Sixola will get him to Managua, then he's on his own."

"Naldo, turn the Hummer around and follow us up. Come on, Perez. Clint saved you from getting to dive through the door to hell."

They waited until the Hummer was backed off the road. Perez went on up, followed by Clint and Ivan. The Hummer came last. At the top, Clint called the number from the slip.

"Habla."

"Dario?"

"No one else would answer this number."

"I'm Clint Faraday."

There was a growing silence. "Uh, I'm sorry. I didn't remember giving you this number. I was a bit drunk."

"Garcia gave it to me."

Another silence.

"Start running, but you won't get far. Here's Ivan." He handed the phone to Ivan.

"Jalisco? ... He hung up."

"Think he'll get away before we get back to Gualaca?"

Ivan quickly punched a number. About three seconds, then, "Code four. Dario Jalisco.

Gualaca." He rang off and handed Clint the phone.

"No."

They headed for Gualaca. Ivan liked the scenery and liked talking with Clint. The Hummer would follow. Perez headed straight for Changuinola as fast as he could go. Clint called two people and they headed back.

Samy left and headed back to the station. He had come to tell Clint a local drunk's body was found on the back road to Guayabal. He would say a tiger tore him up like that – if there were any tigers in the area. A _big_ tiger!

Clint went to sit in his favorite chair to sip his coffee. Tyna came to say they could head back to Quebrada Tula tomorrow. She'd had enough of so-called civilization for awhile.

"I'm too old for this stuff anymore," Clint complained. "I officially retire from detective work. No more!"

"We can celibrate!" Tyna replied. "That's retirement number thirty!"

She sat on Clint's lap and started teasing at him.

"Tyna, I'm too old and tired to keep on with it."

She nuzzled against his neck. He picked her up and headed for the bedroom. "I'm not too old and tired for that!"

C. D. Moulton's works are available on most major outlets as printed or e-books. CD writes the CD Grimes, PI, mysteries, the Det. Lt. Nick Storie mysteries, the Clint Faraday mysteries, the Flight of the Maita science fiction series, books on orchid culture and many others of many types. Mystery, adventure, intrigue, science fiction, humor, fantasy, paranormal, mild erotica, and factual.